HREP

S0-AEE-073

Alone
in the
Forest

Bhajju Shyam
Gita Wolf
Andrea Anastasio

When Musa's
mother fell sick one day,
she couldn't go, as usual,
to fetch firewood from the
nearby forest.

Don't worry, said Musa,
I'm grown up now,
I'll get the wood!

Musa slung his small axe over his shoulder and set off, humming.

It was cool and dark inside the forest, although it was the middle of the afternoon.

Musa picked
his way carefully
through the thorns
and bushes, looking
for the right twigs.

He was
wandering around,
humming to himself,
when something
unexpected
happened.

BOOOOM!

cRA

… out of nowhere,
a great noise came crashing
through the trees.
Musa jumped.
WHAT WAS THAT?
He started to tremble.
He didn't want to look.

The next moment,
he found himself
leaping into the hollow
of a large tree.

His heart beat loudly.
WHAT HORRIBLE
THING WAS THAT?

An awful
thought popped
into his mind:

WILD BOAR!

He'd been chased
by a fierce boar once…
and had never forgotten it.

Now wild boars began
to chase each other,
round and round in
his head.

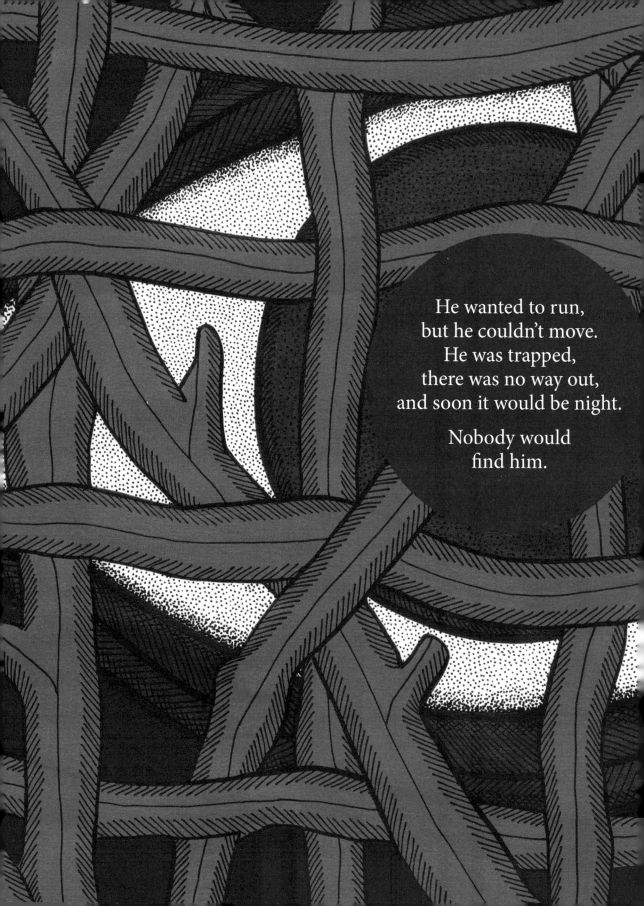

He wanted to run,
but he couldn't move.
He was trapped,
there was no way out,
and soon it would be night.

Nobody would
find him.

Poor Musa. He crouched in the dark hole, ready for something terrible to happen any second. He forgot everything else, and just waited, his heart beating loudly.

He waited...

and he waited...

and he
waited.

After a while, his heart
stopped beating so loudly,
but he still waited,
and then for a while longer...

But nothing happened.

Then at last, after a long, long wh
something finally did happen
Musa's head began to itch.

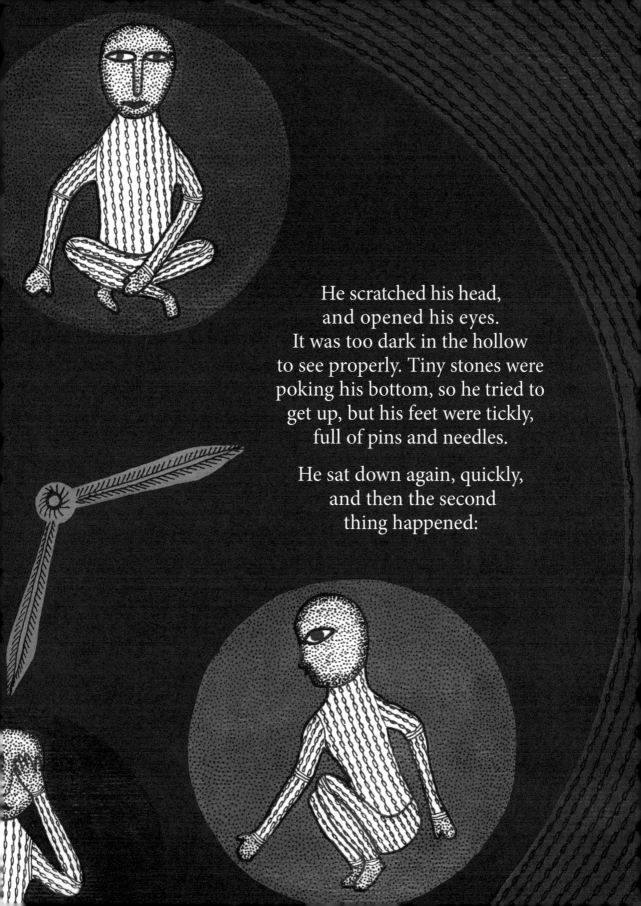

He scratched his head,
and opened his eyes.
It was too dark in the hollow
to see properly. Tiny stones were
poking his bottom, so he tried to
get up, but his feet were tickly,
full of pins and needles.

He sat down again, quickly,
and then the second
thing happened:

He looked up
to see a tiny creature
peeping curiously at him…
it was a squirrel!

Hello, said Musa,
where did you
come from?!

The squirrel ran out of the hollow.

When Musa peered out to see
where she had gone,
the best thing of all happened:

In the bright sunshine outside, he saw a friendly face. It was a cow, ambling along, chewing something.

Musa was delighted. If there is a cow wandering around, he thought, the village can't be far away.

He was safe!

WAIT!
HOLD ON!

Musa called out to the cow,

I'm coming home
with you!

And that's how
Musa managed to return
from the forest that day.

He didn't have any wood,
but he was very proud
of the story he had
to tell.

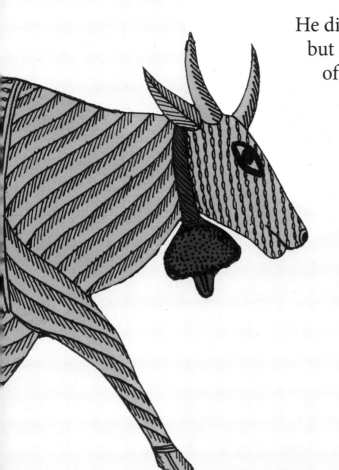

This book has been
illustrated by the well-known
Gond tribal artist Bhajju Shyam,
from Madhya Pradesh in central India.
The Gonds are a community of highly
visual people, who were traditionally
forest dwellers. Their art derives from the
decorative patterns painted on the mud
floors and walls of their houses – it has
now developed into a highly evolved
aesthetic, capable of telling
complex tales.

Alone in the Forest
© Tara Books Pvt.Ltd. 2012

For the text: Gita Wolf & Andrea Anastasio
For the illustrations: Bhajju Shyam
Design: Nia Murphy
For this edition: Tara Books, India, tarabooks.com
& Tara Publishing Ltd., UK, tarabooks.com/uk
Production: C. Arumugam
Printed in China through Asia Pacific Offset

All rights reserved.
No part of this book may be reproduced in any form,
without the prior written permission of the publisher.

ISBN: 978-81-923171-5-1